"I HUMMED A GAY LITTLE TUNE
FOR HIS BENEFIT."

# FAIR TO LOOK UPON

**MARY BELLE FREELEY**

## ITNA

ITNA PRESS
Los Angeles, CA
www.itnapress.com

First published in Chicago, IL by Morrill, Higgins & Co. in 1892.

The ITNA *ICONS* Collection

Original Interior illustrations by W. L. Dodge

Fair to Look Upon by Mary Belle Freeley
ISBN 979-8-9882829-6-9

# CONTENTS

A RIPPLE OF DISSENSION AND WHAT CAME OF IT ..................7

THE STORY OF EVE .........................................11

THE ABRAHAM-HAGAR AFFAIR. ...............................17

ISAAC'S WIFE ..............................................27

A WOMAN'S MONUMENT. .....................................39

ANOTHER OF THE WOMEN OF OLD. ...........................49

ALL NAUGHTY, BUT FAIR. ...................................57

STORY OF SOME WOMEN AND A BABY. ........................63

ANOTHER OF "THE MISTAKES OF MOSES." .....................71

SOME MANAGING WOMEN.....................................79

ANOTHER GROUP OF THEM. ..................................91

THE FAMOUS WIDOW OF MOAB................................99

HE GAVE IT UP TOO. ......................................107

# A RIPPLE OF DISSENSION
# AND WHAT CAME OF IT

I WAS ABOUT to be married. My numerous charms and attractions had won the affections of a young man who was equally charming with myself.

We were sitting on a luxurious divan and he held my milk-white hand in his. I do not make that statement as a startling announcement of an unusual occurrence, but simply as a matter of fact.

We had been conversing about the culinary and domestic arrangements of our future home when matrimony had made us "one flesh;" or, to use English, we had been wondering what under the canopy a good cooking stove would cost, when he asked suddenly and irrelevantly,

"And you will love me, always?"

"Of course," said I, a little impatiently; for when one is deep in a mathematical problem such a question is a little annoying.

"And you will honor me always?" he next inquired.

"As long as you deserve to be honored," I replied, with the habitual good sense of my age and sex, mentally wondering if granite-ware stewpans went with a cooking stove.

"And you will obey me?" he queried next, in a tone that plainly indicated that I'd have to. I left the mathematical problem for future solution and said, hesitatingly:

"Yes—if—I—can."

"If you can?" he said, in sternly questioning tones; and a cloud no bigger than a man's hand appeared upon the heaven of our love.

"I don't believe a woman ever lived who ever obeyed anyone—God, angels, or men," I cried.

"You are a traitor. You slander your sex," he exclaimed, aghast.

"I deny the charge," I replied, springing to my feet, with all the spirit of the above-mentioned age and sex. "By that assertion I only add glory to their fame." He looked at me for a little while, too surprised to speak, and then said, in sarcastic tones:

"Consider our wedding postponed until you have had a little time to study your Bible. Good night."

"'Study your Bible!' That is what everybody says when they want to prove any theory, creed, ism, or anything. I shall study my Bible diligently. Good night," I replied, thinking it was not such very bad advice after all; and then I hummed a gay little tune for his benefit until I heard the hall door close.

And I have studied my Bible with the following result.

# THE STORY OF EVE

AWAY BACK WHEN Adam was a young man—now I know that Adam is rather an ancient subject, but you need not elevate your eyebrows in scorn, for you will be ancient yourself sometime—he found himself in Eden one day; he did not know why, but we do, don't we?

He was there because Eve was to come, and it was a foregone conclusion even in that early age that when she did appear she would want someone to hold her bouquet, open the door for her, button her gloves, tell her she was pretty and sweet and "I never saw a woman like you before," you know.

Her arrival was the greatest event the world has ever known, and the grandest preparations were made for it.

A blue sky arched gloriously over the earth, and sun, moon and stars flashed and circled into space, silvery rivers ran cool and slow through scented valleys, the trees threw cooling shadows on the fresh, damp grass, the birds sang in the rosy dawn, the flowers blushed in odorous silence and yet it was all incomplete, and Adam wandered restlessly around like a man who has lost his collar button.

But suddenly a great hush of expectancy fell upon the world. Not a bird fluttered its feathers, the flowers bowed their heads, the winds and the waters listening ceased their flowing and their blowing, the radiant moonshine mingled its light with the pale pink dawn and a million stars paled their eternal fires, as Eve, the first woman, stood in Eden.

And the world was young and beautiful. The first flush and bloom was on the mountains and the valleys, the birds were thrilled by the sweetness of their own songs, the waves broke into little murmurs of delight at their own liquid beauty, the stars of heaven and the unfading blue were above Adam's head—and yet he wasn't satisfied. Long he stood idly in the brightening dawn wondering why the days were so long and why there were so many of them, when suddenly out from the swinging vines and the swaying foliage Eve came forth.

And though there was a vacant look on her lovely face (for her baby soul had not yet awakened) Adam saw that her lips were red and her arm white and rounded and he whistled a soft, low whistle with a sort of "O-won't-you-stop-a-moment?" cadence in the music, and Eve looked up; and I think at that moment he plucked a flower and offered it to her; and of course she did not understand it all, but Nature, not intelligence, asserted her power, and she reached out her hand and took the rose—and then for the first time in the world a woman blushed and smiled; and I suspect it was at that very moment that "the morning stars first sang together."

Woman has never been obedient. She has always had the germ of the ruler and autocrat in her soul. It was born when Eve first looked with longing eyes at the apple swinging in the sunlight.

While Adam was idly, lazily sunning himself in the garden was Eve contented to smell the fragrance of the violets and bask in the starlight of a new world? Oh no! She was quietly wandering around searching for the Serpent, and when she found him she smiled upon him and he thought the world grew brighter; then she laughed and his subjugation was complete; and then the naughty creature, without waiting for an introduction, led him to the famous apple tree, and standing on her tip-toes, reached up her hands and said with a soul-subduing little pout:

"See, I want that apple, but I can't reach it. Won't you please find a club and knock it off for me?" and she looked out of the corner of her eye and blushed divinely.

Now this Serpent represented, so it has always been believed, a very shrewd person. He saw that this woman had no garments, and that after she had eaten this fruit she would know better, and delight in clothes ever after. So he gave her the apple.

Almost instantly after she had eaten some, not because she particularly liked apples, or had any idea of their adaptability in the way of pies, sauce or cider, but because she wanted to "be as gods knowing good and evil," as the Serpent said she would. Discontent with her wardrobe crept into her heart and ambition for something better sprang to life.

"WHILE ADAM WAS IDLY, LAZILY
SUNNING HIMSELF IN THE GARDEN."

In the distance stood Adam. With a thrill of rapture she beheld him, her aroused soul flashed from her eyes and love was born, and she ran toward him through the flowers, pausing on the river's brink to rest, for weariness had touched her limbs.

She watched the waters running south out of the garden, and like one coming out of a dim, sweet twilight into a blaze of glory she looked and wondered "why" it ran that way, and lo! Thought blossomed like a rose, and generosity laughed in the sunshine when she put the apple in Adam's hand; and Adam, with the only woman in the world beside him, and the first free lunch before him, forgot all about God and His commands and "did eat," and the results prove that free lunches always did demoralize men— and always will. And modesty blushed rosy red when Adam put the apple to his lips, and invention and ingenuity, new-born, rushed to the rescue, and they gathered the fig leaves.

Then memory like a demon whispered in her ear: "The day that ye eat thereof ye shall surely die." She glanced at Adam and deadly fear chilled the joyous blood in her veins. Then she argued: "He will be less angry with me, a woman, and His vengeance will fall less heavily on me than on the man to whom His command was given," and lo! Reason rose like a star on the waves of life, and shoulder to shoulder womanly devotion and heroism that fears neither God nor death in defense of its loved ones entered her soul, and she instructed Adam to say: "The woman tempted me," and deception trembled on her lips when she cried: "The serpent did tempt me," and the tears of regret and remorse watered the seeds of deception and they grew so luxuriously that women have always had that same way of getting out of scrapes ever since.

Yet to Eve belongs the honor of never having obeyed anyone—when it interfered with progress, advancement and intelligence—neither God, angels nor men. The women of the nineteenth century make a profound salaam of admiration and respect to Eve, in whom they recognize the first courageous, undaunted pioneer woman of the world.

# THE ABRAHAM-HAGAR
# AFFAIR.

*"And there was a famine in the land; and Abraham went down to Egypt
to sojourn there."*

YOU SEE ABRAHAM was that charming kind of man—a man
with his pockets full of shekels, for "he was very rich in cattle, in
silver and in gold." So, as provisions grew short in Canaan, and
as in those days when men went on a pleasure trip they took their
wives with them, Sarah accompanied him to Egypt.

Up to this time husbands had only been obedient, but in this
age they began to be complimentary, and as Sarah and Abraham
were about entering Egypt, he said to her, "Behold now, I know
that thou art a fair woman to look upon," and even if it is the first
compliment on record, we must admit, even at this late day, that
Abraham was far advanced in the art of flattery.

Now Sarah was the pioneer, champion, incomparable coquette of the ancient world, and as such deserves our earnest
attention.

We gather from the following events that Abraham realized
her unequaled proclivities for getting in with kings, landlords and
other magnates of the countries through which she was pleasur-
ing, and so he told her to pass herself off as his sister; and because
she believed it would enhance her chances of having a good time,
and as it was easy, natural and agreeable, she did it, and not because she had any idea of merely obeying her husband.

Abraham wanted their marriage kept secret because, in those
days, when a lover-king wished to get rid of an obnoxious husband, he hypnotized him into eternal silence by having him used
as a target for a sling, a spear or javelin, instead of causing an
appeal to the divorce courts, as they do in this civilized and enlightened generation. And I believe that, after all, the old way is
the better one, for when men and women die, they are dead, but
when they are only divorced they are awfully alive sometimes.

"AND THE MEN WATCHED TO
SEE HER GO BY."

And it came to pass, when they arrived in Egypt, the Egyptians "beheld the woman that she was very fair," and the men watched on the street corners to see her go by; and she passed herself as a giddy maiden with such unrivaled success that she gained a notoriety that would have made the fortune of a modern actress, and the princes of Pharaoh commended her wit, beauty and grace to the king, "and the woman was taken into Pharaoh's house."

The attentive reader will observe that Holy Writ, in speaking of a woman, never deigns to say that she is virtuous, industrious, obedient, or a good cook, but seems to ignore everything but the fact that "she was fair to look upon."

That was all that seemed to be required of the "holy women of old."

And Pharaoh "entreated Abraham well for Sarah's sake" (you notice they did everything to please the ladies in those days), and loaded him with riches, presents and honors; and Pharaoh's wives and sub-wives and cadet wives didn't like it. And the Secretary of the Treasury, the Prime Minister and the High Lord Chamberlain of the Bedchamber didn't like it. The neighbors began to talk openly; the scandal "smelled to heaven," and the Lord Himself had to interfere to head the fair Sarah off, and He "plagued Pharaoh and his house with great plagues, because of Sarah, Abraham's wife."

And then—after the preliminary amorous clasping of hands, the little caressing attentions, the lingering kisses; after the fiery expectation and the rapture of possession, after all this came—as it always does—the tragedy of satiety and separation.

"And Abraham went up out of Egypt, he, and his wife and all that he had."

"AND THE WOMAN WAS TAKEN
INTO PHARAOH'S HOUSE."

Yet Peter, in speaking of the duties of wives, has the temerity to refer to the "holy women of old," and holds Sarah up as a bright and shining example for us to follow, saying, "even as Sarah obeyed Abraham, calling him lord." But we won't lay this up against Peter, for it is a telling fact (and shows the predicament he was in) that he had to go back nearly two thousand years to find an obedient woman. There were evidently none in his day, but as he wished to make his teaching effective and submit some proof to clinch his argument, he went back to Sarah and said, "even as Sarah obeyed Abraham," which shows he had never gotten at the real facts in the lovely Sarah's career, or else was misrepresenting Sarah to carry his point in favor of the men.

A careful perusal of my Bible convinces me that the "holy women of old," as Peter dubs them, were all afflicted with a chronic determination to have their own way—and they had it.

But the men were always obedient to the women, and each one "hearkened unto the voice of his wife" and also obeyed God and the angels.

At this point in the history of the affable Sarah and the dutiful Abraham we come to the Abraham-Hagar case, and find the hired-girl question already agitating society.

And the historian tells us that Sarah told Abraham that he could have Hagar for his very own, and then the narrator naively remarks, "And Abraham hearkened unto the voice of his wife."

But of course this is a vile slander against Sarah, and, at this late day, I rise to refute the charge.

Probably some of Abraham's political friends, when the disgrace broke forth in all its rosy glory, trumped up this story about Sarah's consent to save his reputation. But Sarah never did anything of the kind, as her subsequent actions prove. It isn't human nature; it isn't wifely nature; and although Sarah was a little gay-hearted herself, she wasn't going to stand any such nonsense—to speak lightly—from Abraham, and when she discovered his intimacy with the hired girl she quietly called him into the tent, and in less than ten seconds she made his life a howling wilderness. I don't know exactly what she said (as I wasn't there), but it ended, as such scenes usually do end, by the dear man repenting. For, since he is found out, what else can a man do? He said he was sorely tempted, no doubt, and so forth and so on to the end of the chapter, and said: "Thy maid is in thy hands; do unto her as it pleaseth thee." And "Sarah dealt hardly with her, and she fled from her face." But she came back, because you remember she met an angel in the wilderness, and he told her to return. Nice advice from an angel, wasn't it?

The next scene in which the lovely Sarah distinguishes herself, and nobly sustains her record for disobedience and a determination to follow the dictates of her own sweet will, was when Abraham entertained the three angels.

Now hobnobbing with angels wasn't an every-day affair, even in that age when angels were more plentiful than they are now.

And Abraham was naturally a little excited, and he "hastened into the tent unto Sarah," and said: "Make ready quickly three measures of fine meal, knead it, and make cakes upon the hearth," and he gave orders to a young man to kill a calf, etc. And after a while the supper was served, with all the delicacies the rich and great could afford, and everything appeared that he had ordered—except Sarah's cakes. They were simply and inexplicably *non est.*

Of course it was a pretty shabby thing for a woman to go back on her husband in his hour of need, and when there were angels in the house too; but she did it, thereby sustaining her reputation for crookedness and general contrariness as a wife.

And yet it has always been preached to us that we should obey our husbands "even as Sarah obeyed Abraham." Well, we're willing, since all she had to do was to look pretty, be agreeable, and do exactly as she pleased.

But the very fact that Sarah has been held up as an example for us to follow proves that the men had not read up her record intelligently, or else in their extremity they were presuming on our ignorance while trying to enforce order and submission.

But that was not the worst of it. When she heard the angel tell Abraham that she should have a son she ridiculed the idea.

She had the germ of the infidel in her heart, and lacked Abraham's credulity, and would not believe anything, even if an angel did say so, unless it was backed up by reason and common sense, and so she laughed behind their backs.

Now it appears that angels object to being ridiculed as well as other folk, and when they heard her giggling they demanded to know the reason of Abraham. It was exceedingly naughty for her to place her husband in such a predicament, and when she found she was getting the whole family into an uproar she denied the charge, which shows that to her other charming and wifely qualities she added the art of equivocating.

After that Abraham "sojourned in Gerar," and again the seductive Sarah charmed the great king, and again the Lord had to interfere and settle the affair.

When Isaac was born Sarah was more exacting and jealous than ever of Hagar, and said to Abraham: "Cast out this bond-woman and her son; for the son of this bond-woman shall not be heir with my son."

"And the thing was very grievous in Abraham's sight," but he "hearkened unto the voice of his wife," like the dutiful and obedient husband he was, and he sent Hagar and Ishmael out into the wilderness. And even to this day the women who are guilty of Hagar's crime are remorselessly sent out into the wilderness of desertion, despair and disgrace—and it is right and just!

We are told that "fashions change," but Sarah inaugurated a fashion that wives have followed to this day, and will follow till the ocean of eternity shall sweep the island of Time into oblivion.

And so endeth the chapter of the second prominent woman of "Holy Writ."

And Abraham was always "obedient," and "hearkened unto the voice of his wife," and Sarah was a lawless, crafty, coquettish—but never obedient woman.

# ISAAC'S WIFE

AND ABRAHAM SAID unto his servant, "Thou shalt go unto my country and to my kindred, and take a wife unto my son Isaac."

But the servant, who was evidently a student of female character and knew "That when a woman will, she will, You may depend on it; And when she won't, she won't; And there's an end on it," said:

"Peradventure, the woman will not be willing to follow me unto this land."

Then Abraham, who was a connoisseur in feminine ethics (as he naturally would be, having had such able instructors as Sarah and Hagar) and realized the utter futility of attempting to persuade, bribe or induce a woman to do anything she objected to doing, said:

"And if the woman will not be willing to follow thee, then thou shalt be clear from this mine oath."

So the servant departed and "went to Mesopotamia unto the city of Nahor."

Now it seems in those days the girls of Nahor went outside the city gates every evening, according to Oriental custom, to draw water from a well, and the artful servant of Abraham tarried at the well at sunset, for he knew the girls would be along presently.

It was a lovely eventide. The wind touched caressingly the few dainty flowers drooping their heads in sleepy fragrance, the birds twittered soft words of love to their nestling mates, the departing god of day lavished in reckless abandon his wealth of colors; piled crimson mountains red as his ardent love in the western sky, and robed high heaven in golden glory that his sweetheart—the earth—reveling in and remembering the grandeur of his passion and the splendor of his departure, might not love his silver-armored rival of the night.

About this time the maidens tripped down to the well, where the shrewd servant stood as the "daughters of the men of the city came out to draw water," and prayed:

"And let it come to pass that the damsel to whom I shall say, 'Let down thy pitcher, I pray thee, that I may drink,' and she shall say, 'Drink,' may be the one I am looking for," or words to that effect.

The words had hardly passed his lips when Rebekah, with the color snatched from the roses in her cheeks and the grace of untrammeled freedom in her step, skipped down to the well.

And Rebekah "was very fair to look upon." Of course. In relating the history of these examples who have been held up since time immemorial for us to follow, the writers of "Holy Writ" never expatiate upon their virtue, industry, domesticity, constancy or love, but we are simply and briefly told they were "fair to look upon," and the natural logical inference is that we shall "go and do likewise."

Belonging to one of the wealthiest and most influential families of Nahor, of course Rebekah's practiced eye saw at a glance that the handsome fellow waiting at the well and looking the girls over was a person of rank and importance; for it is only a logical conclusion that coming from such a master and bound upon such an errand, he was surrounded by all the trappings and signs of wealth and luxury that the times afforded.

And the maidens of Nahor went outside the city gates partly for the same purpose, I suppose, as that for which the girls of other places go to the parks and matinees nowadays, for it seems to have been a notorious fact that had even spread to other countries, that the girls of Nahor came down to the well in the blushing sunset, and that too, without chaperon or duenna. And I suppose the young men went down too, to flirt with the charming damsels, from the fact that the servant of Abraham tarried there.

And Rebekah, stooping gracefully, filled her pitcher, swung it lightly to her shoulder—and as the woman sometimes takes the initiative in an affair of this kind—smiled upon the willing and ready-looking fellow; not exactly at him, but as it were in his direction, you know; and he caught the faint glint of sunshine on her lips, and then—but in the witching hour when the twilight and sunlight kiss and part, after the smile and look of recognition everyone knows what happens.

And he ran to her and said with the pleasing courtesy of a man of the world:

"Let me, I pray thee, drink a little water of thy pitcher."

Then with the tact of a finished coquette, in three little words she conveyed to him the flattering knowledge that she recognized in him an ambassador of power, wealth and luxury, by saying:

"Drink, my Lord."

After that they became acquainted in the most easy, off-hand manner, without an introduction, and yet we are told to follow the example of these pioneers of the race who were always "fair to look upon."

I never in my life heard priest or people condemning her for forming the acquaintance of a stranger without an introduction; she was called one of the "mothers in Israel," and even St. Paul, who was a regular crank about the girls, classed her with the "holy women of old," which proves he didn't know anything about her history or was playing upon the ignorance of his hearers. She was a leader of the *ton* in Israel, and if in those days they did not banish her from good society, why should we censure the same conduct when we are so much more civilized, enlightened and liberal in our views?

And in an incredibly short space of time he adorned her with earrings and bracelets, and she invited him home with her, and he actually went and made it all right with her mother and big brother by making a prepossessing exhibition of piety, for you remember how he told them "he bowed down his head and worshipped the Lord."

He told them of Isaac, in whose name he sued for Rebekah's fair hand. He didn't say that Isaac was handsome, virtuous, talented or ambitious, but he said, "the Lord hath blessed my master and he is very great; and he hath given him flocks and herds, and silver and gold, and maid servants and men servants, and camels and asses," and unto his son Isaac "hath he given all that he hath," for this astute man of the world seemed to know that the surest and quickest way to win a woman was to show her a golden pathway strewn with the gems of power, luxury and ambition.

And the big brother did not pull out his watch, look at it in a business-like way and say:

"Rebekah, pack your trunk and be ready to take the 6:40 fast express." And her mother did not smile and say, "we're so delighted and honored, I'm sure. Of course she will go." Not at all. They knew better even in those days than to try and coerce or coax a woman to do anything she didn't want to do, and so they simply said:

"We will call the damsel and inquire at her mouth."

Then the servant brought forth jewels of silver and jewels of gold, and raiment, and gave them to Rebekah; and he gave also to her brother and to her mother precious things, and then we are naively told that Rebekah said:

"I will go."

Rebekah was a woman of decision and knew a good thing when she saw it, and so she did not wait to prepare a stunning trousseau or get out wedding cards and invitations fine enough to make all the girls of Nahor sigh in envy and admiration, but she departed at once. Now Isaac was of a poetical nature, and sought the solitude of the fields at eventide to meditate. Like most young men who have a love affair on hand he wanted to be alone and dream dreams and see visions.

And, as good luck would have it, just at this sentimental and opportune moment, Rebekah hove in sight.

And Isaac lifted up his eyes and beheld her; a woman with heaven in her eyes, a mouth sweet enough to make a man forget everything but the roses of life, and a form seductive enough to tempt the very gods from on high.

And she beheld a man, young and strong and handsome, the touch of whose hand opened the gates of glory to her soul, "and she became his wife, and he loved her," thereby putting himself on record as the first man in the world we have any sacred official notification of as having loved his wife.

So the days and months, brightened by smiles and tarnished by tears, dropped into the wreck-strewn, motionless ocean of the past, and in the course of human events two little boys played marbles in the tent of Isaac, and Rebekah scored the rather doubtful distinction of going on record as the first woman who ever doubled expectations and presented her husband with twins.

At this period the fair Rebekah begins to get in her work as a disobedient wife, a deceitful, intriguing woman and an-all-round-have-her-own-way variety of her sex.

"Isaac loved Esau, but Rebekah loved Jacob," and we conclude from that, as well as from the actual facts in the case, that there were domestic tornadoes, conjugal cyclones and general unpleasantness all round. About this time there was another famine in the land and Isaac and Rebekah (and others) went into the land of the Philistines to dwell, and of course Rebekah's beauty attracted universal attention, and the men of the place questioned Isaac about her and he replied that she was his sister, as he said, "lest the men of the place should kill me for Rebekah," because she *was* fair to look upon.

In that age it appears when a man fell in love with a woman he killed her husband, instead of hoodwinking and outwitting him as they do in this progressive era, but I suppose in spite of the awful chance of losing her husband by some sudden and tragic death, Rebekah slyly and seductively smiled upon "the men of the place" from the fact that a little farther on we read that the King issued a mandate, saying:

"He that toucheth this man or his wife shall surely be put to death."

The King knew that Isaac was favored of the Lord, and he was afraid of some swift and condign punishment if Isaac became offended by the amorous attentions of any of his subjects to Rebekah, so he gave the order to the men.

You will readily discern by that command that he was a keen and intelligent student of female character, and knew there was no use or reason in appealing to her sense of justice, her obedience to, or respect for law, or her regard for the "eternal fitness of things" in a case of the affections, and so he appealed to the fear and obedience of the men, for he realized that no man's pleading, no King's command, no threats from heaven or fears of hell can stop a woman's coquetry.

A little farther on Esau went the way of all young men and married, and worse than that he married Judith the daughter of a Hittite, "which was a grief of mind unto Rebekah and Isaac."

We know that one of Rebekah's strongest points was putting herself on record for doing something that no woman ever did before that we have any authorized statement of, and she did it in this case by being the first woman who hated her daughter-in-law.'

As we read on we find she was not the meek, submissive and obedient wife we are told women should be.

She systematically and continually had her own way, in spite of husband, sons, kings, men, God or angels.

"AND REBEKAH WAS—A WOMAN."

We discover that by a succession of deceptions, tricks and chicanery she cheated Esau out of his blessing, obtained it for Jacob, and deceived and deluded her dying husband, all at one fell swoop.

It is but just to Jacob to say that he objected to putting himself in his brother's place, but Rebekah said, "only obey my voice," and he obeyed—of course.

The men were always obedient, as the Bible proves conclusively. They obeyed everybody and anybody—kings, mothers, wives, sweethearts and courtesans.

But where can we find any evidence of the vaunted obedience of woman?

Not among the prominent women of the Bible at least.

Rebekah influenced her husband in all matters, advanced one son's interests and balked another's aims, prospects and ambitions. In short she played her cards with such consummate skill that she captured everything she cared to take.

Jacob was obedient, complimentary, submissive and loving and Rebekah was—a woman.

# A WOMAN'S MONUMENT.

*"And there came two angels to Sodom, at even."*

NOW LOT AND his wife were residents of Sodom, and they entertained in the most courteous and hospitable manner the angels who were the advance guards of the destruction that was about to sweep the cities of Sodom and Gomorrah into oblivion, leaving only a blazing ash-strewn tradition to scare the slumbers of the wicked, and stalk a warning specter down the paths of iniquity through unborn ages.

And the softening twilight fell upon the doomed but unconscious cities. Unpitying Nature smiled joyously. The cruel sun, possibly knowing the secret of the angels, gayly flaunted his myriad colors, and disappeared in a blaze of glory without wasting one regret upon the wicked cities he would see no more forever.

No angelic hand wrote in blazing letters one word of warning across the star-gemmed scroll of heaven; but the song rung out on the evening breezes, laughter rose and fell and the red wine flowed; women danced lightly on the brink of destruction and men jested on the edge of the grave.

And yet some rumor of these angels and their errand must have reached the fated cities, for after Lot had dined and wined them before they retired, "the men of the city, even the men of Sodom, compassed the house round, both old and young, all the people from every quarter."

And Lot went out and tried to pacify them, but his eloquence and his pleading were in vain, and they said, "Stand back." And they said again, "This one fellow came in to sojourn, and he will needs be a judge."

"AND LOT WENT OUT AND TRIED
TO PACIFY THEM."

And I imagine there was a great tumult and confusion, angry
words, flashing eyes and an ominous surging to and fro, "and they
pressed sore upon the man, even Lot," but still he pleaded the
defense of the angels, and meanly offered to bring out his two
young daughters and give to the howling mob—but the passion
that glowed in the eyes and trembled in the voices of the raging
throng was not a passion to be allayed by the clasp of a woman's
hand, the flash of her azure eye, or the touch of her lips; and besides, that boisterous, angry crowd evidently did not believe in the
efficacy of vicarious atonement and they flouted the offer. The
uproar increased, curses and maledictions rung out, the demand
for the men grew louder and louder, and at this perilous moment
the angels "put forth their hand and pulled Lot into the house to
them, and shut to the door," and "They smote the men that were
at the door of the house with blindness, both small and great: so
that they wearied themselves to find the door."

And in that crushing moment when eternal darkness fell upon the multitude the cries of anger and revenge died away, and such a moan of anguish and despair burst upon the affrighted night that the very stars in heaven trembled.

Then the angels confided to Lot their dread secret and told him to warn all his relatives to leave the city with him, and he went out and told his sons-in-law of the impending calamity, and he "seemed as one that mocked unto his sons-in-law."

The morning came blue-eyed and blushing, and the angels hastened Lot and his wife, and hurried them out of the city, saying, "Escape for thy life: look not behind thee, neither stay thou in all the plains: escape to the mountains, lest thou be consumed."

Now if there were any more disreputable people in the cities than Lot's two young daughters, we don't wonder that the vengeance of a just God sent a blasting storm of bursting flames to lick with their fiery tongues these wicked cities from the face of the earth. What does arouse our wonder is that those fair girls with the devil's instincts smouldering in their hearts should be allowed to escape the general baking. But excuse us; our business is to state facts and not to wonder or surmise.

From subsequent facts we suppose that Lot's wife sadly, perhaps rebelliously, lingered, for we find the angels saying again:

"Haste thee, escape thither; for I cannot do anything till thou come thither," and they escaped to the city of Zoar, "and the sun was risen upon the face of the earth when Lot entered into Zoar."

"Then the Lord rained upon Sodom and Gomorrah brimstone and fire from the Lord out of heaven."

But before the end Lot's "wife looked back from behind him and she became a pillar of salt."

All the information we have of Mrs. Lot is exceedingly meager; only one short sentence and two little clauses in other sentences; and yet no figure of history, no creation of a poet's dream or artist's brush since the world, wrapped in the laces of the twilight and the mists, and rocked in the cradle of the first early morning of life, until the present day, old in experience, wrinkled with care, heart-sick with too much knowledge and laughing without mirth, stands out more clearly before the world than Lot's wife—and why?

Because it has been supposed that she was very naughty.

In this world it is the wicked folks who get the glory and the everlasting fame; the good people get the snubs, the crumbs, the eternal oblivion.

The whole history of Lot's wife lies in the fact that she was told by the angel of the Lord to do one thing, and she—didn't do it.

But that is characteristic of the women of old; they systematically didn't do it if they were told to, and systematically did do it if they were told not to.

And Madam Lot "became a pillar of salt," because of her disobedience, and has stood through the centuries a warning statue to naughty females; yes, more than that, for she has seemed a criminal whom just vengeance caught in the very act and turned into a pillar of salt, standing in the plain near Sodom, against a background of shame, crime and punishment, that the eyes of the world of women might look upon forever, and be afraid.

But in this day and age we are beginning to see that in Lot's wife it was a case of mistaken identity, and instead of being a criminal she was a great and good woman, and although the "pillar of salt" commemorates an act of dire disobedience, it also extols a loving heart and a brave act.

Just imagine her position. She was leaving her home, around which a woman's heart clings as the vine clings to the oak, her children, her friends; breaking the ties that years of association and friendship had woven about her in chains of gold, and leaving them to a terrible fate. But stronger than all these gossamer, yet almost unbreakable threads, was the love she bore her husband; a love so intense, so deep that it made her obey a command of God's against which every instinct, passion and emotion of her nature rebelled.

He was going and her daughters were going with him, and womanlike she forsook everything to follow him—the man she loved; the man whose frown could make her heart sore as the wounds of death and agony, and her heaven dark with the clouds of desolation and despair; or whose gentle smile or caressing touch could sweep the mists of doubt and uncertainty from her mind, even as June kisses make June roses blossom, her weary eye glow with the light that love alone can kindle, and clothe rough labor in robes of splendor.

Softly the dawn awoke, gayly fell the sunlight on the doomed cities, and joyously the breezes swept the plains round about Sodom and Gomorrah.

And Lot and his wife and daughters obeyed the command: "Escape for thy life; look not behind thee, neither stay thou in all the plains; escape to the mountains lest thou be consumed."

And now with frantic haste Lot's wife urges them on; she even leads the way in her mad desire for their escape, encouraging them by word, look and action. And while her heart is a battle-ground where a desperate conflict is raging, there is no hint of disobedience or rebellion in her eyes, no lagging in her footstep, no tears for love, no sighs for friendship, no backward glance of compassion toward the wicked but dear city.

And now they have come a long way—and suddenly the sunshine grows dark, the wind falls, flutters, dies away; then comes the ominous hush that foretells the bursting storm.

And this woman knows that her daughters and her husband, the lover of her youth and the lover of later years, in short the one loved lover of her life, is safe; safe from the tempest of destruction, safe from the wrath of God. A wave of joy floods her heart at the thought. No harm can touch them; she revels in that assurance for a moment—and then she forgets them.

The white-capped breakers of disobedience against the cruel command "look not behind thee" sweep with crushing force across her soul; the unjust command that stifles compassion. All the angels and demons, the joys and sorrows of life, urge her to turn back; love of children, friendship of old neighbors, regret for the joys that have fled, remorse for the wicked deeds she has done, the unkind words she has spoken, a blind unreasoning rebellion against the fate that has overtaken her friends and home, fight against God's command. And in that awful moment when the furious winds strike her like angry hands, when Fear levels his glittering dagger at her heart, Death holds his gleaming sword before her eyes, the heavens disappear, hell sits enthroned in fiery flames upon the clouds; above the deafening roar of the maddened tempest the crashing thunder that made the very dead tremble in the corruption of their graves, and the awful surging of the blazing rain, she heard God's command ringing out "Look not behind thee."

For an instant she paused to cast an ineffable smile of love upon the cherished ones at her side, and then before the eyes of unborn millions, while all the hosts of heaven and even God himself stood appalled at her daring, she slowly and deliberately turned and looked back; and that one glance showed her a sight that froze her into a beautiful statue of disobedience, love and compassion.

She was loving, tender, daring—but disobedient!

Oh, that we might find one woman in the Old Testament meek and humble, to whom we could pin a faith, not born of teaching and preaching and general belief, that such a thing as a submissive, obedient, tractable woman or wife ever did exist.

# ANOTHER OF THE WOMEN OF OLD.

AT THE COMMAND of his mother, let it be remembered, and not because he had any particular desire to do so himself, Jacob left home and departed unto the land of his mother's people, where she told him to seek a wife.

The life of many men of the Old Testament (after they have reached man's estate, I mean) begins with a love affair, and I infer from that, that the Bible means to teach the lesson that to love is the first and best business of life, as well as the most entertaining and pleasant thing that this world ever did or ever will have to offer.

And Jacob reached the land of Laban, his mother's brother, and stopped by a well where the flocks were watered. This is the second well which figures conspicuously in a love story of the Bible, and we imagine they were the trysting places of the ancient young lovers.

While Jacob was loitering and gossiping with the young men he found there, "and while he yet spake with them, Rachel came with her father's sheep; for she kept them."

Now "Rachel was beauteous and well favored," and of course Jacob saw all this at a glance, for a man never yet needed a telescope and a week's time to decide whether a woman possessed the elements which constituted beauty in his mind or not, and so Jacob gallantly rolled the stone away from the well and watered the flock of Laban, and then, with all the boldness which characterized his future notorious career, he "kissed Rachel, and lifted up his voice and wept."

As there could hardly be anything but pleasure in kissing a lovely maiden, we naturally infer that Jacob was very emotional and was crying for effect, and that Rachel, with the consummate tact that all the women of the Bible displayed when managing the men, perfectly understood this, and had as little respect for him at the moment as most women have for a tearful man. A man like Jacob cries easily, and when he thus "lifted up his voice and wept," it is to be hoped the girl entirely understood him.

And Jacob's kiss is the first one that love ever pressed upon the lips of a blushing maid—at least it is the first one that is authoritatively recorded.

At that time Jacob started a fashion that "custom cannot stale," a fashion that while time lasts shall be as cheap as roses, laughter and sunshine, as thrilling as wine, as sweet as innocence and as new as love, a fashion that wealth, time or country cannot monopolize, and one that is as sweet to the beggar, and sweeter too, than to the king.

At the end of one short month we find him so desperately enamored that he said to Laban, Rachel's father: "I will serve thee seven years for thy younger daughter," and the old gentleman, seeing an opportunity to get a hired man cheap, consented.

"And Jacob served seven years for Rachel, and they seemed unto him but a few days for the love he had to her."

What a world of devotion that one sentence reveals. As we read that we forget all about the prosaic age in which we live; forget the modern I'll-give-you-a-brown-stone-front-and-dia-monds-in-exchange-for-your-youth-and-beauty-love, and believe in the kind that makes a man a god and a woman an angel, and we imagine that an affection so intense and deep that it could make seven weary years of labor "seem but a few days" must be as constant as the flowing tide, as steadfast as the stars—and then after a while we are desperately, despairingly sorry that we have read any further than that verse because we are so sadly disillusioned.

## "AND JACOB SERVED SEVEN YEARS FOR RACHEL."

For a little further on we find that Jacob wasn't as shrewd about getting married as he was about breeding cattle that were ring-streaked and grizzled, and so Laban, with the cunning of a modern politician, palmed off his daughter Leah on Jacob as a bride. But the next morning, when he discovered the trick, there were probably matinees, side-shows and circuses in the tent of Laban, and finally the upshot of the whole affair was that he agreed to serve seven years more for Rachel, and then married her also. Far be it from me to disparage Jacob's love, but we cannot help but notice that we have no inspired statement saying that the seven years he served for Rachel, after he had married her, "seemed but a few days for the love he had to her."

But we can't censure him for that, for as we read we discover that in his earnest and constant endeavor to save his precious person he had no time to nurture his love. For the two wives, the two sisters, were madly jealous of each other of course (and we can't blame them either, for there never was a man so great that he could be divided between two wives, several handmaids and more concubines, and be enough of him to go around satisfactorily) and they made his life a howling wilderness.

Leah, poor thing, longed for her fraudulent husband's love, and he hated her. Rachel "envied her sister," and "Jacob's anger was kindled against Rachel," and altogether the picture of their home is not very enticing, and having gotten thus far we are more than ever convinced that we do not want to follow the example of the "holy women" of old, as Peter complimentarily, but ignorantly, calls them.

And Rachel and Leah, in order to spite and humble each other, each gave her maid "to Jacob to wife" and strange as it may seem, he accepted them both. It was like him.

Now about this time Leah's son "found mandrakes in the field" and brought them to his mother. We suppose Rachel had a sweet tooth from the fact that a little further on we find her offering to sell her husband for one night to Leah, for some mandrakes, whatever they were; and we notice that women held their husbands rather cheap in those good old days.

You see Rachel and Leah made Jacob a thing of barter and sale and (without consulting his desires) Leah consummated the bargain, and she went out toward the field when the harvest was progressing, and met Jacob as he came from his work tired and dusty, and informed him he must come with her, "For surely I have hired thee with my son's mandrakes," and he did not resent the insulting idea that he had been "hired," but like all the other distractingly obedient men of the Bible—he went.

Rachel next distinguishes herself as a disobedient daughter and headstrong wife by "stealing her father's gods" without consulting or confiding in her husband, for we read that "Jacob knew not that Rachel had stolen them."

And Laban, Rachel's father, and Jacob had a lively altercation, and they said exceedingly naughty things to each other in loud voices, but at last they came to an agreement, and Laban said he would give up his children, grandchildren and cattle, but he was bound to have his "gods" or know the reason why. The entire story is a curious mixture of heathenism and belief in one God.

Then Jacob rose in all the confidence of perfect innocence and told him he might search the whole camp for all he cared, and he added in his outraged dignity, "with whomsoever thou findest thy gods, let him not live."

You will observe by that that it was a terrible crime to steal "gods," and as it is the first offense of the kind on record, you can infer what a reckless, ungovernable female Rachel must have been to do so dreadful an act.

Well, Laban went like a cyclone "unto Jacob's tent" (notice what humiliation and disgrace Rachel subjected her husband to, and what a scandal it must have raised in the neighborhood), and into Leah's tent and into the two maid-servants' tents; but he found them not. Then he entered into Rachel's tent.

Now she had hidden the precious little images in the camel's furniture and sat upon them, and she said she didn't feel very well this morning, papa dear, or words to that effect, and she hoped he would excuse her for not arising; and she probably smiled sweetly, put her arm around his neck, and finally did him up completely by kissing him tenderly; and of course, as in those days men never dreamed of asking a woman to do anything she didn't want to do, papa dear did not insist upon her arising, and so missed his sole and only chance of getting his "gods."

It was a very serious and perhaps terrible loss to her father, and we can gather no idea from the scripture why she did it unless out of pure spite, or else she wanted to use them as bric-a-brac in the new home to which she was going.

In the history of the "beauteous and well-favored" Rachel and the "tender-eyed" Leah, we find hatred, deadly jealousy, anger, strife, dissensions and envy, but none of the forbearance, self-sacrifice, obedience, meekness and submission that we have been taught that the ladies of the Old Testament possessed, and we are almost sorry that we didn't take the preacher's "say so" for it, instead of studying the Bible diligently and intelligently for ourselves.

# ALL NAUGHTY, BUT FAIR.

THE NEXT YOUNG lady whom the Old Testament presents for our admiration and edification is Dinah, the daughter of Jacob and Leah, who set the passionate but agonizing style of "loving not wisely, but too well," and brought about one of the shrewdest military stratagems that was ever perpetrated, a terrible massacre, and the slavery of many innocent women and children.

Several other ladies are mentioned casually and then we come to Tamar, whose father-in-law, Judah, had broken his solemn promise and defrauded her of her rights. And did she submissively consent to be deprived of her just dues? Not at all. She simply disguised herself, and by deception and a thorough knowledge of man's nature, mixed up with a shrewd business tact, completely out-generaled her dear papa-in-law, gained her revenge, and by a sagacious artifice protected herself from the possible consequences of her folly and from future punishment by persuading Judah to give her, as a pledge of his good faith, "his signet and bracelets and staff." In short, she was the original pawn-broker of the world; and Judah left his treasures "in escrow" until he could redeem them by delivering her a kid in liquidation of his debt.

And for many days the sun blazed and faded, the stars sparkled and paled, and the moon rode high in silvery radiance; the winds and birds and flowers blushed and sang and sighed, and in due course of time Judah sent a kid to redeem his valuables, but alas! Tamar had slipped away and left no trace by which she could be identified, and Judah, who had broken his pledge, was left in suspense.

But finally the time of retribution came, as come it does and must to every possessor of a pawn ticket. The days, those bright beads on the rosary of time, were counted one by one and shadows began to gather about the fair name of Tamar. Then the whispers of suspicion grew to pealing thunders of scandal which reached and shocked the good Judah, and he rose up in his moral rectitude and righteous indignation at such depravity and cried:

"Bring her forth and let her be burnt."

But my lady, with a woman's wit, had foreseen this possible denouncement and punishment, and prepared for it, and she quietly sent the articles he had left in pawn, and humbled him to the very dust with her message.

"Discern, I pray thee, whose are these, the signet and bracelets and staff?" And I will add here that there was no fire, because Tamar skillfully avoided being the fuel.

I do not relate the above to harrow up your feelings, but simply to show you the stuff the women of the Old Testament were made of.

About this time the matchless Joseph appears upon the stage of the Old Testament as the monument of masculine virtue, and lo! the woman in the case enters upon the scene in the shape of Potiphar's wife, and plays her part in the comedy or tragedy—as you happen to look at it—in Joseph's life.

She doesn't come before the public with a burst of melody, a blaze of light and the enticing music of applause, but she enters softly, quietly she "casts her eyes upon Joseph" and she sees he is "a goodly person and well favored"—and the mischief is done. She lavished her wealth in all the follies, fashions and pleasures of her time to attract him; she met him in the hall, gave him roses in the garden, smiled at him from the doorway. When she slept she dreamed sweet dreams of kisses and soft hand-clasps. When she lifted her gaze to the stars, 'twas his eyes she saw there. When she walked by the river's side, the rippling waters were no sweeter than his voice. When the summer wind, perfume-laden, fanned her face she fancied 'twas his warm breath on her cheek. Then she forgot husband and duty, heaven and hell, and she listened for his footsteps, lingered for his coming, watched and waited for his smile—and all in vain.

And Joseph, who loved this woman with an incomparable love; this woman who from the eminence of her wealth, rank and beauty, in the utter abandonment of her passion cast herself at his feet, Joseph was man enough to bend and sway and falter before her temptations, but for friendship's sake, for honor's sake, for the sake of her he loved, divine enough to resist them.

Out from among the seductive fables and shocking facts of history Joseph stands forth a shining example as the first man, and perhaps the last, who loved a woman so well that he refused her outstretched arms, declined the kisses from her lips, rejected the reckless invitation in her eyes, and saved her from himself. Who loved with a passion so tender and deep that, unlike all other men, he refused to make her he loved a victim on the altar of his passions, but would have enshrined her there a goddess, "pure as ice and chaste as snow."

Men have always sacrificed women "who loved not wisely, but too well" upon the altar of their own selfishness, but Joseph saved her and taught the world what true love is.

The facts of history stab our faith in man's love, woman's constancy, friendship, honor and truth, but Joseph's peerless example revives it, and we feel that there are characters that are incorruptible, honesty that is unassailable, virtue that is impregnable and friendship that is undying. He shines out from among the other characters of the Old Testament as distinctly and clearly as a star breaking through the sullen clouds of heaven, as a lily blowing and floating above the green scum and sluggish waters, as a rose blooming in a wilderness. Thank the Lord for Joseph!

But Potiphar's wife, womanlike, scorned a love that would make her an angel instead of a victim, and by a succession of plausible, neat little lies, gained her husband's ear, had Joseph cast into prison, and teaches us that, indeed, "Hell hath no fury like a woman scorned."

But what we wanted to say was, that she was a faithless wife, a reckless lover, a revengeful and unforgiving woman, since Joseph was left to languish in captivity for two long years, without any effort on her part, as far as we can learn or infer, to accomplish his release.

At this period in the history of the Jews a new king arose in Egypt, and fearing the great number of the Jews, he "set over them task-masters, to afflict them with their burdens," "but the more they afflicted them the more they multiplied and grew."

Then the king, in the usual arrogance of power, ignorantly supposing that women were obedient and never dreaming they would dare to disregard the commands of royalty, spoke to the Hebrew midwives, and in the easy, off-hand manner that kings had in those days, told them to kill all the boy babies that came to the Jews, but to save the girl babies alive.

And did they do it? Not at all! They simply looked at each other, laughed at the king, and utterly ignored his commands, and then when majesty in dread power called them to account, with a shrewdness characteristic of the females of the Old Testament they invented a plausible excuse, baffled the king, shielded the Jews and saved themselves.

# STORY OF SOME WOMEN AND A BABY.

SO THE KING was balked by the Hebrew midwives and the Jews continued to "increase abundantly and multiplied, and waxed exceeding mighty; and the land was filled with them."

And the king, fearing the multitude of the Jews, again pitted himself against the fecundity and rebellion of the women, and issued the cruel but famous command:

"And Pharaoh charged all the people, saying, Every son that is born ye shall cast into the river, and every daughter ye shall save alive."

And shortly after that, one night when all the Egyptians slept, and only the stars, the moon and the winds were awake, in the silence and the silvery gloom, a baby boy came to a daughter of Levi, and "when she saw him that he was a goodly child" she quietly determined that no murderous hand should ever toss him in the rolling river, or check the breath on his sweet lips; "and she hid him three months."

I don't know how she did it, but perhaps when he was crying with all a baby's vigor for his supper the embryo diplomat in his heart shrewdly caught the meaning in his mother's warning "hush, sh!" and, king and tyrant tho' he was, he knew "that there was a greater than he," and stilled his cries. Perhaps when the colic gripped his vitals he bore the pain in unflinching silence, if he heard an Egyptian footstep near the door. Perhaps he stopped his gooing and cooing in his hidden nest, and held his very breath in fear, when he heard an Egyptian voice in the house.

And all these three months he had been growing plump, and strong and healthy, and I suppose he became a little reckless, or perchance he began to think he knew more than his mother did about it, and wouldn't keep still. Anyway, whatever was the matter I don't know, but there came a day when "she could no longer hide him," and then she laid a plot to baffle the king, defeat death and save the child.

Being an ambitious woman as well as a loving mother, she was not content that he should be as other children, forced "to serve with rigor" and his life made "bitter with hard bondage in mortar and brick and in all manner of service of the field." I presume she thought he was a little more beautiful and more clever than any child that ever lived before, for we all do that when a baby comes without an invitation and often against our most urgent wishes, and nestling in our arms says, without uttering a word: "I've come to stay and I want my supper; I'm hungry, for the journey has been long and dark—and why don't you make haste?"

Perhaps she had caught the fire of the future statesman in his dark eye; perhaps she had heard the ring of sublimity in the melodious voice that afterward said "Honor thy father and thy mother." Perhaps she had seen the shrewdness of the future great diplomat in his maneuvers to have his baby way, and being a bright woman she set her wits to work to defy the king, defeat his law and elude the cruel vigilance of the Egyptian spies; and she conceived a plot which for boldness of thought and shrewdness of execution stands unsurpassed. She would not save him to live the toilsome, slavish life of the Jews. She sighed for all the advantages of the Egyptians. She lifted her ambitious eyes to the royal household itself, and in spite of the accident of birth, in spite of king and law and hatred, in spite of the fatal fact that he was a dark-eyed, dark-haired Jew, she vowed he should mingle with royal nabobs, laugh and thrive and prosper under the very eye of his enemy the king, be clothed in purple and fine linen, skilled in all the arts and learned in all the sciences of the Egyptians; and she was clever enough to see at a glance that in this almost hopeless scheme she must have accomplices.

And where did she turn for aid? To her husband, as a meek, submissive and obedient woman naturally would? Not at all. Perhaps she doubted the intelligence of his assistance. Perhaps she had no faith in his courage for the undertaking. Perhaps she did not believe he could keep a secret; at any rate she refused to confide in him. I suppose, as no mention is made of it, she utterly ignored him, scorned to ask his advice, and planned to dispose of his child without telling him of it, much less asking his permission.

But where did she turn for aid? Did she clothe herself in the gayest costume of the Jews, and, conscious of her beauty, try with smiles and coquetry and caressing touch to beguile the King? No. Did she steal into the tent of his greatest general and kneeling at his feet seek to bribe him with her love? No. She simply and utterly ignored the men, and selected the King's own daughter as the instrument to execute her design. She knew the royal girl came down to the river to bathe, and trusting in her baby's great gift of unrivaled beauty and the woman's compassion, she planned a dramatic surprise for her.

"And when she could not longer hide him, she took him an ark of bulrushes, and daubed it with slime and pitch and put the child therein. And she laid it among the flags by the river's brink." But before she put him in it she bathed him in perfumed water to make him sweet, put on his prettiest dress, tied up his short sleeves with something that just matched the color in his cheeks, and borrowed a golden chain of an Egyptian woman to clasp about his milk-white neck. Then she lined the ark with roses, laid a little pillow in the bottom, put the baby softly in, partly closed the top to shield him from too much light and air, and laid it among the flags by the river's brink; and then the cleverness that had designed the scheme and the bravery that had executed it so far, was overwhelmed by a mother's love and she fled, and hid herself among the foliage and the reeds, too frightened to watch the result; "but his sister stood afar off to wit what would be done to him."

And the baby had a nice time while he waited, for the wind with noiseless feet and invisible hands came and softly rocked the cradle to and fro; the sunbeams sent a bright ray and put golden bracelets on his wrists, which with the true instinct of human nature he tried to catch and hold, and the birds coming down to wash in the rippling waters peeped into the cradle, and, enraptured with the pretty sight, forgot to bathe, but stopped to sing.

And the King's daughter and her maidens came laughing and singing down to the river's brink to bathe, as was their custom— a custom which the baby's mother knew about and took advantage of.

And the girls spied the basket and wondered what it was, and finally the royal damsel "sent her maid to fetch it." And Pharaoh's daughter opened it and "she saw the child," and the girls crowded around and gazed in silent admiration. Then the baby, who never before had seen the purple and fine linen of majesty or the sparkling jewels of wealth, knowing this was the opportunity of his life put up his hands in welcome and said in the universal language of babyhood, "Ah, goo! ah, goo!" He was a worthy child of a great mother, and the minute he was left to himself he came before the footlights and with one word captivated his audience, and a storm of kisses fell upon his lips and neck and arms. And when the girls ceased lest they should kiss him to death, he looked at them a minute, and then he opened his mouth and laughed a little soft, gurgling laugh; a laugh so sweet that I'm sure even the terrible God of the Jews must have smiled had he heard it.

He didn't laugh because he felt particularly funny, but because the little diplomat, bent on conquest, wanted to show a tiny tooth that came into his mouth one day, he didn't know how.

He had never seen it himself, but he knew it was there and was a treasure, for one time in the dead of the night when all his dread enemies, the Egyptians, were fast asleep, and the wind howled and the rain beat upon the roof, his mother brought his father to his hiding place and holding the light high up above his head, she touched him lightly under the chin and said: "Laugh, now, and show papa baby's tooth." Then he did as he was told and his father looked long and carefully and then laughed too, kissed him and went away.

When the girls saw it they all smiled and kissed him too.

About this time he wanted his mother and "the babe wept."

When the king's daughter saw his red lips quivering and the tears hanging on his long, curling lashes, love and compassion filled her heart, and thinking of her father's wicked command: "Every son that is born ye shall cast into the river," she said, sadly, "this is one of the Hebrews' children."

Then his sister—I suppose it was the same one who had "stood afar off to wit what would be done to him," and who had approached—said, "Shall I go and call to thee a nurse of the Hebrew women, that she may nurse the child for thee?"

"And Pharaoh's daughter said to her, 'Go.' And the maid went and called the child's mother."

"And Pharaoh's daughter said unto her, 'Take this child away and nurse it for me and I will give thee thy wages.' And the woman took the child and nursed it." Wasn't that the sublimest conquering of ambition and crime by love ever known?

I suppose the King's daughter went every day to see the little black-eyed beauty and kiss his rosy lips, his soft white neck, his dimpled arms; and every kiss strengthened her determination to defy the King, her father and the law, and save this baby for her own.

I don't know how she managed it, but somehow she overcame all obstacles, and they were many and great there is no doubt, and "he became her son," and the future lawgiver of the Jews, and the world was saved.

And so after all we owe the ten commandments to a Jewish woman's wit, strategy and love, and an Egyptian woman's compassion and disobedience, for the stern command that "Every son that is born ye shall cast into the river" was not given to the army, the navy or the church, to one man or woman, to doctors or midwives, but to "all the people," and in this affair there were a number of women, who all connived to foil the "powers that be" and refused to do the King's bidding. First there was the mother of Moses and the sister, the King's daughter, her maid and "her maidens" who came down to the river brink with her, at least two of them and perhaps twenty.

I fail to find in their example any of the vaunted submission, obedience and docility we have been taught by those who did not read their Bible intelligently, or took some other person's "say-so" for it, and which are the vaunted characteristics of all these women.

They just simply scorned all the men and the laws whenever they did not suit their ideas of right and justice, and proceeded to have their own way in spite of everything.

# ANOTHER OF "THE
# MISTAKES OF MOSES."

*"And it came to pass in those days, when Moses was grown, that he went out unto his brethren and looked on their burdens, and he spied an Egyptian smiting an Hebrew, one of his brethren. And he looked this way and that way, and when he saw that there was no man, he slew the Egyptian, and hid him in the sand."*

YET WE ARE told a little farther on, "Now the man Moses was very meek, above all the men which were upon the face of the earth." But we haven't anything to do with his meekness, and only mention the murder because thereby hangs the tale of Moses' first love affair.

"Murder will out," and so in due course of time the King heard about it and "sought to slay Moses." "But Moses fled from the face of Pharaoh, and dwelt in the land of Midian, and he sat down by a well."

Now when we read about the young men of the Bible hanging around a "well" we know what is going to happen. There is romance in the air and a love affair soon develops, for that seems to have been love's trysting place. And I suppose he neglected no artifice of the toilet that might enhance his personal charms, that he donned the most costly and elegant of his Egyptian costumes, flung himself in courtly indolence upon the sand, and waited and watched eagerly for the rich girls to come down to the well to water their father's flocks, just as one watches in the twilight for the first star to sparkle in the azure overhead, for the first sunbeam of the morning or the first rose of June.

"Now the priest of Midian had seven daughters, and they came and drew water and filled the troughs to water their father's flock. And the shepherds came and drove them away, but Moses stood up and helped them, and watered their flock."

And who can blame Moses if he happened to wear his best raiment? Everything and everybody knows, and always has known, that love loves the beautiful; and each one according to his light takes advantage of the fact. So the wild maiden, when love with magic finger touches her quivering heart, stains her teeth a blacker black, hangs more beads and shells about her dirty neck and ankles, and practices all her rude arts of coquetry. And her savage lover, charmed with her charms, sticks the gayest feathers in his hair, rubs a more liberal supply of grease upon his polished, shiny skin, and makes himself brave with all his weapons of war. So the birds only seek love's trysting place in the springtime when their plumage is the most brilliant and their songs the sweetest, and the fishes when their colors are the brightest. And the woman of our day and generation, when love's arrow "tipped with a jewel and shot from a golden string" pierces her vital organ, wears her dress a little more décolleté, bangs her hair more bangy, clasps more diamonds round her throat, dispenses with sleeves altogether, smiles her sweetest smile and laughs her gayest laugh. And he, the modern man, caught in the snare, buys the shiniest stovepipe hat and nobbiest cane, dons his gaudiest neck-tie and widest trousers—and after all, beasts and birds and fishes, savage and civilized, we are all alike and ruled by the same instinct and passion, and "why should the spirit of mortal be proud?"

I presume Zipporah, one of the priest's daughters, had heard about the elegant and courtly Egyptian who was in the neighborhood, and she no doubt adorned herself with all her jewels, wore the finest finery in her wardrobe and wreathed her lips in smiles; for she knew that love lives and thrives on smiles and roses, coquetry and gallantry, on laughter and sweet glances, and faints and dies on frowns, neglect and angry words; and so she tripped down to the well, bent on conquest. Then she flung back the drapery to show her dimpled arms, and drawing water filled the trough; then the "shepherds came and drove them away; but Moses stood up and helped them, and watered their flocks." Was he not gallant, and a striking contrast to the ugly shepherds?

And of course Moses told her that it almost broke his heart to see her performing such menial labor, and all such sweet fictitious stuff, and she glanced at him admiringly from under her long, curling lashes, and the "rebel rose hue dyed her cheek," and he told her about the great court where he had been reared, and she whispered that her papa was the rich priest of Midian; then they clasped hands lingeringly and said a soft goodnight.

It seems the old gentleman kept a pretty close watch on his girls—and he doubtless had a steady job—for he asked them how it happened that they had returned so soon. And Zipporah put her arms around his neck, and placing her cheek against his told him all about the gallant and courteous stranger. Having an eye to business—as behooves a father with seven daughters on his hands—he didn't let this eligible young person slip, but sent and invited him to his house and deluged him with hospitality and kindness—and Moses and Zipporah were married "and Moses was content to dwell with the man."

But after a while, first soft and low and then in trumpet tones, ambition whispered in his ear that he could deliver the Hebrews from their enemies. "And Moses took his wife and sons and set them upon an ass, and he returned to the land of Egypt."

And I suppose, though time was young and wore roses then, the days passed slowly to Zipporah and she grew tired of Moses and the Lord, tired of the rod that turned into a serpent, of the strife and the bondage and the river of blood; tired of the frogs and the lice and the swarms of flies; disgusted with the murrain of beasts and the boils and terrified at the thunder and fire and rain of hail and all the horrors of Egypt, and like the woman of to-day, when things get too awfully unpleasant, she made it uncomfortable for Moses, and "he sent her back" to her father's house and she took her two sons with her.

Afterward when Moses became famous and illustrious she returned to him without asking his consent, or even notifying him of her intention, as far as we can learn from the official records.

She took her father, the priest Jethro, along to look after her and take care of her baggage I suppose, and we imagine he didn't relish the task much, for we hear him saying, rather apologetically we think, "I, thy father-in-law Jethro, am come unto thee, and thy wife, and her two sons with her."

I fancy Moses knew the condition of a man who was in the clutches of a woman, and that woman his wife, so he forgave the old man, for he had experience himself, "and went out to meet his father-in-law, and did obeisance, and kissed him; and they asked each other of their welfare." But there isn't any record that he kissed his wife, or even shook hands with her, and we infer that their domestic heaven was not all blue and cloudless.

Miriam, although a prophetess and a sister of Aaron, wasn't very angelic, at least the glimpses we catch of her don't impress us with the fact that she was. When the seashore was strewn with the dead, white faces of the drowned Egyptians, and the waves were flecked with their pallor and dashed their helpless arms about, Miriam "took a timbrel in her hand: and all the woman went out after her with timbrels and with dances." And Miriam answered them, "Sing ye to the Lord, for he hath triumphed gloriously: the horse and his rider hath he thrown into the sea."

Now this may have been natural and all right for the times, only you know it doesn't look well when compared with the action of our women of to-day, who drop tears and roses on the graves of their enemies.

Further on we find Miriam, womanlike, talking about Moses because he had married an Ethiopian woman, and saying seditiously to Aaron, "Hath the Lord indeed spoken only by Moses? hath he not spoken also by us?"

And the Lord heard it and his anger "was kindled against them," and my lady "became leprous, white as snow."

As she was the one punished for daring to talk rebellion against Moses, God's chosen one, we suppose she was the ringleader and instigator, and Aaron was only the tool in this plot that budded but never bloomed.

"And Aaron looked upon Miriam, and behold, she was leprous," and of course she threw her arms around his neck and with streaming eyes besought his aid, and Aaron turned the smoothly flowing river of his eloquence into resistless words of appeal and said unto Moses, while Miriam knelt at his feet: "Alas, my Lord, I beseech thee, lay not the sin upon us," and "let her not be as one dead," and Moses, moved, as men have always been moved, by woman's tears, "cried unto the Lord, saying, Heal her now, O, God I beseech thee," and after seven days the curse was removed.

# SOME MANAGING WOMEN

THE WOMEN OF the Old Testament always wanted something, and it is a noticeable fact that they always asked for it—and got it too.

So the daughters of Zelophehad had a grievance, and they didn't go among the neighbors bewailing their hard lot, they didn't sit and wish from morning till night that something would turn up to help them, or sigh their lives away in secret, but they put on their most radiant attire and jauntiest veils and "stood before Moses, and before Eleazar the priest, and before the princes and all the congregation," and demanded their father's possessions, and even argued the question reasonably and logically. There was not any of the St. Paul-women-should-not-speak-in-meeting doctrine about the Biblical women of those elder days.

They didn't endeavor to persuade Moses' wife to influence her husband to use his power on their behalf. They did not retain the services of Aaron, the finest orator of the day, to plead their cause, but they did their own talking, and they got what they asked for— their father's possessions—and husbands thrown in without extra charge. Being clever as well as ambitious women, they probably foresaw that husbands would follow after the inheritance, and although they would not ask for lords and masters of course, they had their eyes on them just the same. As there were several of them, all unmarried, they were no doubt *not* "fair to look upon," so they laid a little plot to secure husbands. And they succeeded and were happy, for marriage was the aim and end of a woman's existence then, and there was a better market and more of a demand for husbands than in these modern days.

We only catch a glimpse of one woman named Achsah, but that is enough to show us that she possessed the prevailing and prominent characteristic of all the other "holy women."—she wanted something.

After she had married her warrior lover, who conquered Kirpathsepher for her sweet sake, the very first thing we find is that "she moved him to ask of her father a field." Now naturally a young man would dislike to approach his father-in-law upon such a delicate subject, and so soon too, but *she* asked him and he obeyed—like all the men of the Old Testament.

And even then she was not satisfied; but of course she embraced her father and kissed him, and told him he was the most indulgent father in the whole wide world.

Now Caleb no doubt had had dozens of love affairs, and experience had made him a connoisseur of female character, and understanding all their little scheming ways and little designing tricks, without beating around the bush at all he came to business at once and asked,

"What would'st thou?"

"Give me a blessing; for thou hast given me a south land, give me also springs of water," she said.

Springs of water were a bonanza in those days—something like a gold or silver mine to us moderns—but she had requested it and of course he could not refuse, "and he gave her the upper springs and the nether springs."

And it came to pass that Joshua sent two men, two spies, saying, "Go view the land, even Jericho," and I suppose they disguised themselves and went by secret ways; anyway they eluded the vigilance of their enemies and entered the city, even Jericho, and let me whisper it in your ear, they went to see a woman named Rahab—and she wasn't a very nice woman either—and "lodged there."

But their visit leaked out, as such things always do and always will, though the stars should pale their fires to shield them, the moon withdraw behind the clouds to hide their shadows, the rain pour and the thunder crash to drown their footsteps. Perhaps the children told the neighbors, perhaps the hired girl whispered to her friend, perhaps some jealous watching lover told of it, but at any rate we read:

"And it was told to the King of Jericho, saying: Behold there came two men in hither to-night of the children of Israel, to search out the country."

"And the King of Jericho sent unto Rahab, saying: Bring forth the men that are come to thee, which are entered into thy house: for they be come to search all the country."

Now does one suppose for a moment that she obeyed the mandate of the King? Of course not, if one is a student of the Bible, but if one is not, I'll just say that she took them up through the skylight and hid them, piling flax over them, and then she said innocently and convincingly to the King's officers:

"There came two men unto me, but I wist not whence they were: And it came to pass about the time of shutting of the gate, when it was dark, that the men went out: pursue after them quickly; for ye shall overtake them."

Then she went up on the roof and talked to the men like a lawyer. I notice that these old women—I mean women of old— were all good talkers, and they didn't speak like meek, passive, submissive girls wrought up to sudden action by wrong, indignation or revenge, but they spoke with a freedom, vigor and fluency that betokened everyday practice.

St. Paul says that woman should "Keep silence," and that "they are commanded to be under obedience," but he evidently had some remarkable ideas upon this and other topics. Perhaps he never had read the official records, and we know he was never married, and so we don't censure him so much for his ignorance of female character, having never had a wife, or, so far as we know, a love affair, for what does a man born blind know about the sunshine, or the lightning's awful flash, or one born deaf know of the pealing, clashing thunder?

The women of his day were no doubt obstreperous and extravagant, and hence his famous but perfectly ineffectual teaching that they should not "broider their hair, or wear gold or silver or costly array," and that they shouldn't talk in meeting, and if they wanted to know anything, ask their husbands, and drink of their intellectual superiority. But to return.

So Rahab made the spies swear that when the doom of destruction fell upon Jericho, she and her father and mother and all her relations-in-law should be saved, and then she let them down from the window of her house, which was very conveniently built upon the town wall, with a scarlet rope.

So you see, by deceit, strategy, disobedience and a succession of neat little lies, she thwarted the King, betrayed the city, and saved her own precious self all at one fell swoop.

When the walls of Jericho fell and childhood in its innocence, ambitious manhood, fiery youth, despairing maidens and loving mothers, were swept by maddening flames and glittering swords into the oblivion called death, from whose silent gloom no smile or tear, no laughter or wail, ever yet has come, then Rahab and all that she had was saved. She had asked it, and schemed for it, and of course she did not fail.

Next we come to Deborah, a prophetess, who judged Israel at that time, and from the little that is said of her husband, we infer she was the head of the house and ruled him besides attending to her professional duties.

Well, Deborah sent for Barak and commanded him to meet "Sisera, the captain of Jabin's army," in battle array. But he was afraid, and to inspire him by her courageous example she went with him to the field of battle, and every man of Jabin's host "fell upon the edge of the sword; and there was not a man left." But Sisera "fled away on his feet" to Jael, the wife of his friend. Sisera, like another defeated general, had lost his horse.

And she went out to meet him, and gained his entire confidence by smiles and deception, and took him into her tent and gave him milk to drink, covered him with a mantle, and said in her sweetest tones, "Fear not." Then when he slept the sleep of perfect exhaustion, defeat and despair, she "took a nail of the tent, and a hammer in her hand," and softly, with bated breath and step that often paused and ear that bent to listen, she approached him, and then—quicker than the lightning's flash or tiger's spring "she smote the nail into his temples, and fastened it into the ground: and he was fast asleep and weary. So he died."

Nice way for a woman to treat her husband's friend, wasn't it?

Abimelech killed seventy of his brothers to become King, and after wars and battles too numerous to mention he came to "Thebez, and encamped against Thebez, and took it." But there was a strong and mighty tower in the city and a thousand men and women, stained with blood, expecting no mercy, but defiant to the last, fled there for a few hours of safety.

"And Abimelech came unto the tower and fought against it, and went hard unto the door of the tower to burn it with fire."

And all the men stood aghast, helpless and despairing, waiting a terrible death. Then a woman with a vision of blood and moans, dying men and ravished women before her, with a courage born of desperation and a wit sharpened with intense fear, boldly stepped to the window ledge, and in the glare of bursting flames and the sound of dying groans "cast a piece of a millstone upon Abimelech's head, and all to break his skull."

"Then he called hastily unto the young man his armour-bearer, and said unto him, Draw thy sword, and slay me, that men say not of me, A woman slew me. And his young man thrust him through, and he died," as a man naturally would who had been hit on the head with a millstone and pierced through with a sword; and every one in the tower was saved.

I'm not telling you this to harrow up your feelings, but just to show you that the holy women of old were not such nonentities as some of us have supposed.

And time, undelayed by the roses of June or the snows of winter, by sunshine or starshine, by laughter or sighs, by birth or death, hurried on and the Jews fought and triumphed, bled and died "and did evil, and the Lord delivered them into the hands of the Philistines." And after a while Samson was born, and what do you suppose he did just as soon as he became a man? Why he went down to Timnath and fell deeply, desperately, madly, in love with a Philistine girl, and he went straight home and told his father and mother about it and they did not approve of it—they never do, it seems—but he was determined to have her, for there was not another female for him in the whole wide world—they all think that for the time being—and of course he married her. Then he made a seven-day feast, and unfortunately he amused the company with a riddle. Of course his wife was dying to know the answer, and her people threatened her if she did not find it out, and altogether it was a lively discussion, and she made his life a burden and a delusion and she wept before him and said:

"Thou dost but hate me and lovest me not; thou hast put forth a riddle unto the children of my people and hast not told it to me." And Samson declared he hadn't told it to his father or mother or any living soul and swore he would not tell *her*—but he did. For "she wept before him the seven days while the feast lasted," and on the seventh day, exhausted by her upbraidings, deluged by her tears and wearied by her everlasting persistence, he whispered it in her ear, and she told the children of her people.

It is safe to conclude that Samson was angry, and the wedding feast broke up in confusion and dismay, and he went and killed thirty people, and the woman who had "pleased him well" he repudiated with such dispatch that it suggests Idaho and the modern man, and "Samson's wife was given to his companion, whom he had used as a friend." The views we get of married life and the domestic relations in the Old Testament make us almost think that marriage was a failure—in those days.

Then Samson, after a little affair which I do not care to dwell upon with a woman of Gaza, who was no better than she should have been, fell blindly in love with Delilah. And, being in love, he profited not by his late experience (what man or woman ever does who is in love?) and again he told the dearest secret of his heart to a woman, because, forsooth, "she pressed him daily with her words, and urged him, so that his soul was vexed unto death." And then with her fine arms around his neck and her kisses on his lips, he fell asleep on her knees—and she betrayed him.

# ANOTHER GROUP
# OF THEM.

THE GREAT ARRAY of the Philistines "came and pitched in Shunem, and Saul gathered all Israel together, and they pitched in Gilboa," and unseen by any of the mighty hosts death and rapine, treachery, revenge and murder, smilingly waited for the desperate battle.

Then Saul, gazing upon the great army of his enemies and terrified at the countless thousands, thought he would like to have his fortune told and said, "Seek me a woman that hath a familiar spirit," and they took him to the witch of Endor, and Saul prayed her to materialize Samuel for his especial benefit. And did she do it? Not at all, or at least not until she had made her own conditions. "And Saul sware to her by the Lord, saying: as the Lord liveth, there shall no punishment happen to you for this thing." And then having brought the King to terms, by cunning hocus-pocus she summoned Samuel from the cold, cold grave. First there was a hush, then a sweeping in of chill, damp air, a scent of decay, the shaking out of a shroud that never rustled, a rush of silent footsteps, and suddenly the door untouched swung noise-lessly open and Samuel, with the old regal air, but with the savor of death clothing him like a mantle, and the mildew of death on his brow, stood before them.

You will observe he was far too courteous a ghost to censure a woman—who really was the one who deserved it, since she had wrought the mischief—but said sternly to Saul:

"Why hast thou disquieted me, to bring me up?"

The inference is that after all his triumphs and defeats, his loves and illusions, his glory and fall, he was taking the sweet and silent rest of utter oblivion, and very naturally he did not like to be disturbed, and so he told Saul some things that very nearly scared the lingering hope out of him, and almost reduced him to a condition where he himself was a fit candidate for a compan-ionship with Samuel. Then suddenly the air grew warmer and fresher, the birds began to twitter in the first faint flush of the morning, and looking around one could not see Samuel anymore.

Then the witch of Endor wanted Saul to take some refresh-ment, "But he refused and said, I will not eat."

But the woman did not pay any attention to his refusal, but killed a calf and cooked it, and made some biscuits "and she brought it before Saul, and before his servants, and they did eat" of course, since she smilingly invited them to.

We suppose Saul's wife—at least one of them—was a lady who carried things with a high hand, ruled the servants, nagged her husband, delivered curtain lectures by the hour, scolded him to sleep and then scolded him awake again.

"And whipped the children, and fed the fowls, And made his home resound with howls," since we hear him saying to his son Jonathan, "Thou son of the perverse, rebellious woman."

And behold Saul and David were the firmest friends, and every act of David's pleased Saul, and every smile delighted him, and Saul honored, trusted and advanced him, until the women came to have a hand in the affair and then all was changed.

It seems that no one had noticed, or dared to give voice to the thought, that David was becoming a dangerous rival of the great King, until the women, with keen penetration, looking upon the handsome David, saw there was a greater one than Saul. And so one day when David returned from a great slaughter of the Philistines, the girls came and danced and sung and waved their white hands and smiled, and despite the probable indignation of the King at the open preference and approval of the young man, they played and said, "Saul hath slain his thousands, and David his ten thousands."

And Saul was jealous and "very wroth" and—well, that ended that friendship, and it wasn't the last time that women's smiles and honeyed words of praise have blighted the friendship between men "whose souls were knit together."

And there was a woman whose name was Bathsheba, and she was very beautiful. Her midnight hair curled softly away from her snowy brow, her long black lashes hiding her love-lit eyes swept her rosy cheeks, and her light step dashed the dew from the grass in the garden, while the blossoms fell from the boughs to kiss her shoulders as she passed.

And one eventide, David, walking upon the roof of his palace, saw her bathing. And the last red rays of the sinking sun touched her softly and changed her into a perfect statue of warm pink marble, and David's soul was ravished by her beauty; and with the impetuosity of a king and the reckless passion of a lover he sought to beguile her. And Bathsheba, flattered by the preference of the mighty King, allured by imperial grandeur and enticed by royal appeals, tried to forget the husband, who was off to the wars and away, and who had in the first flush of youth won her by his love, his "brow of truth" and a soul untouched by sin—but the King— the King, the pomp and the power!

Ambition was roused in her heart and she wanted to be clothed in the purple and fine linen of majesty, and to wear a jeweled crown upon her brow. And so she forgot a husband's love, a wife's honor, a woman's virtue, and while angels wept and devils laughed, the memory of Uriah vanished from her mind as a star vanishes before the fire-bursting storm-cloud.

Then black-browed conspiracy and red-handed murder, the boon companions of unholy love, whispered in their ears; and though a vision of Uriah often rose unbidden and unwelcome before her, it was dimmed and obscured by the glitter of jewels and the gleam of costly array, that should yet flash upon her arms and throat and clothe her limbs.

So David sent for Uriah (we presume with the consent, perhaps at the instigation of Bathsheba, for there is no wickedness like the wickedness of an ambitious, faithless wife), honored and feasted him, and the favored young man, happily unconscious of his wife's treachery, perhaps dreaming bright waking dreams of the wealth, fame and power he would win to lay at Bathsheba's feet, felt himself honored by being made a special envoy to carry a letter from the King to his greatest general, Joab—and in it the King wrote:

"Set ye Uriah in the forefront of the hottest battle, and retire ye from him, that he may be smitten and die," and Joab "assigned Uriah unto a place where he knew the valiant men were," and he was smitten and died.

And David and Bathsheba were married, but surely, as they stood by the cradle of the little boy who died, the cold hands of the valiant, betrayed Uriah must often have pushed them asunder, and a dark shadow born of their guilty hearts must have passed between them and the child. Perhaps when the feast was the gayest a battle field rose before them, and when the music was the loudest and the sweetest, thrilling through it, they heard a dying moan.

When Joab wanted to reconcile David to Absalom, he wished a mediator with wit, tact and delicacy; with the eloquence of an orator and the subtle flattery of a Decius Brutus, and whom did he choose? A man? No: He sent for "a wise woman," and we read that he instructed her what to do, but judging from other women we are sure she instructed him—anyway she went to the King, and she talked like a lawyer, she plead with eloquence, she confessed charmingly, and she flattered with the cunning of her sex, saying, "for as an angel of God, so is my Lord the King to discern good and bad," and "my Lord is wise, according to the wisdom of an angel of God," which you will admit was putting it pretty strong. But then, men who didn't work for their living in those days were used to strong language—of praise. Perhaps it is superfluous for me to add that the "wise woman" accomplished her mission.

We are told in poetic language that David "was ruddy, and withal of a beautiful countenance, and goodly to look to," and perhaps that was the chief reason (although women always adored a man of valor, intelligence and strength) that "Michal, Saul's daughter, loved David," and thus gave him the proud distinction of being the first man who was ever loved by a woman—at least the first one we have any authentic, official record of.

Once upon a time David had prepared to wipe Nabal, who was a very rich man, and his followers, from the very face of the earth, because a young man "told Abigail, Nabal's wife, saying, Behold, David sent messengers out of the wilderness, to salute our master, and he railed on them."

Nabal was a churlish miser and little to be trusted, and it seems Abigail, who "was a woman of good understanding and of a beautiful countenance," had heard nothing of this little affair, but she was equal to the emergency and she at once prepared many presents of wine, and figs, and raisins and other good things, and made haste to go out and meet David, and if possible avert the impending calamity. "And she said unto her servants, Go on before me; behold I come after you. But she told not her husband," which shows conclusively that although he was "churlish and evil in his doings" she was not under his dominion to any great extent, or afraid of his anger, for she took things in her own hands and ran the government to suit herself, for the time being at least.

So she met David, made a telling speech, pleaded eloquently, flattered skillfully, and David, who never could withstand the beauty and oratory of another man's wife, granted her every request, as he himself confessed and said (I notice David always got particularly pious when he was going to do or had done anything particularly mean) to Abigail:

"Blessed be the Lord God of Israel which sent thee this day to meet me: and blessed be thy advice."

I don't know what kind of bargain they had made, but it sounds a little queer to hear him saying to her, "go up in peace to thine house; see, I have hearkened to thy voice and have accepted thy person."

Abigail returned home and found her husband had been having a gay time while she was away, and "his heart was merry within him, for he was very drunken," so she waited till the morning "when the wine had gone out of Nabal," as it is quaintly put, and then she "told him these things," but as there was nothing but good news in "these things" she must have told him something else that is not recorded, for "his heart died within him, and he became as stone."

Now, I wouldn't cast a suspicion on Abigail for any consideration, but it does seem a little strange that ten days after her memorable meeting with the handsome and musical David, "the Lord smote Nabal that he died."

"And David sent and communed with Abigail, to take her to him to wife."

I simply mention this little romance to prove that there was no evidence of obedience in Abigail's conjugal relations.

# THE FAMOUS WIDOW
# OF MOAB.

AND NAOMI, WEARY of the land of Moab, in the shadows of whose mountains, guarded by the angel of eternal sleep, lay the graves of her husband and sons, longed in her loneliness for the friends and associations of her youth. Her heart turned back to the old house at home, where there is always more sunshine and starshine, softer breezes and sweeter birdsongs, more silvery streams and fragrant flowers, than in any other clime, and she was about to take her departure for the "land of Judah."

Now it seems that Naomi was a very loveable elderly lady, since her daughter-in-law seemed to like her very much, though I haven't the slightest idea that Ruth was really so madly in love with her as we have been taught to believe.

It appears that back in the "land of Judah," Naomi had a kinsman of her husband's, "a mighty man of wealth of the family of Elimelech; and his name was Boaz."

You know it is true that when we go to live in a strange country, we tell our new acquaintances, incidentally and casually, perhaps, but we tell them just the same, about our wealthy and famous relatives, while the names of those who were hanged because they may have loved horse flesh "not wisely but too well," were arrested for gambling, eloped with some other woman's husband, or made garden on shares for the neighbors, are kept locked in our hearts as too sacred to mention to curious ears. Of course Naomi was no exception, and so Ruth had often listened, spellbound, to Naomi's description of this "mighty man of wealth," of his fields undulating in golden waves, far and near; of the springs that gushed and sparkled and flowed down the hillsides; of the shining streams idly wandering in his verdant valleys, whose blue waves rose to caress the flowers on the bank that dipped to be kissed; of his costly array, his men servants and maid servants and all the show and grandeur that was his.

So Ruth went down to the river one day and gazed at her own reflection in the liquid depths, took an honest inventory of her charms, and the pride and confidence of the embryo conqueror thrilled her veins, the rose hue of triumph dyed her dark cheek, and knowing that Boaz was, according to the law of the Jews, her future husband—if she could please him—she went back and said to Naomi with the inherent eloquence of a brilliant widow bent on conquest:

"Entreat me not to leave thee, or return from following after thee; for whither thou goest, I will go; and where thou lodgest, I will lodge; thy people shall be my people, and thy God my God:

"Where thou diest, will I die, and there will I be buried. The Lord do so to me, and more also, if aught but death part thee and me."

And Naomi, the dear old lady, was very much flattered and had perfect confidence in her daughter-in-law's professions, and so do we also believe her words—that is, moderately.

When she says, "thy people shall be *my* people," we believe she meant it—as far as Boaz was concerned at least; but when she adds "thy God shall be my God"—well, we have known many people who were quite pious when they were about to do something they wished to cover up, and their prayers were a little more fervent at that time, just to throw people off the track, so to speak. And Ruth had decided to capture Boaz's heart with her midnight eyes, wear his gems upon her breast, and plunge both hands deep down in his golden shekels. But of course she didn't intend to confide this dead secret to a garrulous old lady, and have it reach the ears of the mighty man of wealth perhaps, for the cunning, witty, pretty widow knew that a man never likes to be caught.

So one day she (with Naomi) arrived at Bethlehem with a half a dozen things in her favor, any one of which would have made her noted, at least.

She had youth (she was not more than twenty-eight perhaps) the divine gift of beauty, the luck of being a stranger, the advantage of being a widow, the prestige of a convert, and the novel notoriety of being the first woman in the world who ever was in love with her mother-in-law.

Is it any wonder "that all the city was moved about them?"

Well, no doubt Ruth found out all she wanted to know about Boaz, learned his habits and characteristics, made all the inquiries she wished in a way that "was childlike and bland," and at last having her arsenal well armored with the big guns of wit and beauty and garrisoned by facts and observations and the experience of an ex-wife, she was ready for Love's war, where the bullets are soft glances, the sword thrusts kisses and the dungeon of the captive is the bridal chamber, and she went to her mamma-in-law and said sweetly, "let me go now to the field and glean ears of corn after him (you see she admitted she was after him) in whose sight I shall find grace."

"And she went, and came, and gleaned in the field after the reapers; and her hap was to light on a part of the field belonging unto Boaz." Wonderful, wasn't it, that it was her "hap" to light on a part of the field belonging to Boaz?

FAIR TO LOOK UPON · 103

And lo, in the morning ere the sun was halfway up the blue sky, Boaz came into the barley field and his eyes fell upon the beauteous Ruth gleaning with the reapers, and delighted at the sight, he called the general manager and said:

"Whose damsel is this?" And he answered and said: "It is the Moabitish maiden that came back with Naomi out of the country of Moab."

It seems Boaz had never seen her before, although her fame had reached his ears, and he spoke to her softly and kindly, praised her for her devotion to her mother-in-law (you see that captured his fancy and admiration, as it has everyone's since), and then she smiled and thanked him very ardently, and then the wily widow turned her pretty head aside and blushed. And Boaz, who had never heard the advice to "beware of the vidders," was taken in and done for in that one short interview. He hung around the fields, deserted the city, cared naught for its pleasures, forgot the dames of high degree, and lingered for hours among the reapers to catch a glance from her dark eye, or a smile from her ruby lips, and I suppose they sometimes rested in the shade and talked sweet nonsense, or sat in the intoxicating silence when love speaks unutterable things to the heart alone, and the "old sweet story was told again" in the harvest field near Bethlehem.

"Boaz commanded his young men saying, Let her glean even among the sheaves, and reproach her not: And let fall also some of the handfuls of purpose for her, and leave them, and rebuke her not."

Having alighted upon an easy task, Ruth knew it. "So she kept fast by the maidens of Boaz to glean unto the end of barley harvest and of wheat harvest: and dwelt with her mother-in-law."

And yet it seems the gentleman did not propose. So Naomi and Ruth talked it over together, for by this time his infatuation was the talk of the city, and sentimental, romantic old Naomi, who must have been a charming woman in her day, was interested in this love affair. For no matter how old a woman or man may be, the perennial stream of love and sentiment flows on in the heart, although hid 'neath white hairs and wrinkles, and bound by the wintry shackles of age and custom; still it is there, and often breaks the icy barriers of the years and betrays itself by a late marriage, or in the matchmaking proclivities of all elderly women.

And Naomi gave Ruth some instructions which we blush to think of, but she followed them implicitly. And the middle-aged Boaz was caught. We suppose he was forty-five or fifty from the fact that he called Ruth "my daughter," and commended her because she didn't run after the gilded youths of society, but preferred him above them all. And Boaz and Ruth were married, and like most marriages between widows and old bachelors it proved a happy one.

But Ruth's shrewd scheming and successful venture as related in the inspired records confirms our belief that it was Boaz the "mighty man of wealth," and not Naomi's love or Naomi's God that induced Ruth to emigrate to the city of Bethlehem.

We are told that Jezebel, unknown to her husband, "wrote letters in her husband's name and sealed them with his seals," and had a man stoned to death without his knowledge, not the man's, but her husband's.

That doesn't look as if she were ruled over much, does it?

The sacred history says, speaking of Hagar and Ishmael, "and his mother took him a wife out of Egypt" which means that she selected the girl and told him to marry her—and he obeyed. And we find that Solomon gave to the queen of Sheba "whatsoever she asked," which is an example of generosity we would recommend to the men of to-day.

# HE GAVE IT UP TOO.

I HAD REACHED this point in my study of the Bible, when one evening, just as I had seated myself to begin work and was idly sharpening my pencil, the door bell rang.

I had not seen my lover for weeks; not since he had so sarcastically advised me to peruse the Scriptures. I had waited for his coming, but in vain; the mail brought no letter; he sent no word by friend or foe. And I made no sign. His had been the fault and his should be the reparation, and so a profound silence fell like a pall between us.

But love, the god of gods, strung the invisible wires of mental telegraphy between our hearts, and over the mystic, unseen lines our thoughts, bright as hope, dark as sin, lighter than the thistle down, heavily charged with the electricity of doubt and trust, faith and fear, love and longing, flew noiselessly back and forth through the stillness and drew us unconsciously together; and so it happened that he stood upon the doorstep and pulled the bell.

There was always a triumphant peal to his ring that seemed to say to my heart, "Lo, the conquering hero comes." And now that vital organ bounded gladly in my breast, then stood still; my pulses throbbed with delight and triumph. Ten minutes before I would have thrown the world away, if it had been mine, for one smile from his lips, but now—I seized my pencil and wrote rapidly on the tablet on my knee as he entered the hall, came into the room, and stood beside me, then with a little start I looked up and exclaimed in feigned surprise:

"You here?"

"I think I am," he said, "but if you want me to, I'll look in the mirror to make sure." And then we both laughed, for 'tis so easy to laugh when one is happy and all the world is gay.

"Well," said he, sitting down beside me, clasping my hand in his as lovers sometimes do, and taking up the conversation where it had been dropped weeks and weeks before, "they say you can buy a good cooking stove for forty dollars—and I've had my salary raised ten dollars a month."

Then I smiled and he said abruptly:

"When are you going to marry me?"

"I haven't completed my study of the Bible yet, and I don't think I could be submissive, and——"

"Oh, fiddlesticks!" he exclaimed, impolitely interrupting me, "I don't want you to be submissive; I just want you to love me and—and—boss me," he added, in the very depth of repentance.

"But you demanded obedience," I insisted.

"I was foolish then," he said softly, "but absence from you and silence has taught me wisdom. When I left you and you made no sign, sent no word of recall, left the dread quiet unbroken, I told myself that you cared nothing for me, and I tried desperately to fall in love with some other girl, but they were all 'flat, stale and unprofitable' compared to you. There was no light in their eyes, no roses on their cheeks, no pleasure in their presence, no rapture in their touch—and—Oh, hang it! you know I can't talk, but I love you, and as long as cooking stoves and marriage licenses are so cheap and ministers are so plenty what's the matter with having a wedding tomorrow?"

And I said—but never mind what I said.

# BOOKS BY ITNA

*Urban Gothic: The Complete Stories*
Bruce Benderson

*Bruno's Conversion*
Tsipi Keller

*Aaron's Rod*
D. H. Lawrence

*The Beads*
David McConnell

*The Virtuous Ones*
Christopher Stoddard

*After David*
Catherine Texier